CONTENTS

Snailsleap Lane

Grizzles at home in his garden

Snailsleap Lane

by
BESHLIE

Hart-Davis and Gallery Five

To Jan, David and Angela,
my friends at Gallery Five

Granada Publishing Limited
First published in Great Britain 1977 by
Hart-Davis Educational Limited
Frogmore, St. Albans, Hertfordshire
and Gallery Five Limited, 14 Ogle Street, London W1P 7LG

Illustrations Copyright © 1973, 1974, 1976 and 1977 Gallery Five Limited
Text Copyright © 1977 Gallery Five Limited.
Layout by Daphne Mattingly

ISBN 0247 128 384

Colour Reproduction by Carlton Repro. International Ltd., Winchester.
Printed in Great Britain by William Clowes & Sons, Limited,
London, Beccles and Colchester

He saw the thin figure of a Shrew coming along the lane

GRIZZLES THE VOLE HAS AN ENCOUNTER

Grizzles, the short-tailed Field Vole was in a thoughtful mood. The winding pathway from Up and Along Crossing to Romany Wood, and known to all as Snailsleap Lane, was as clean as a new pin. Not a scrap of unsightly rubbish spoilt the fringe of blue Forget-me-not, pink Vetch or white Barren Strawberry.

This was just as well, for Grizzles was responsible for keeping the road clear. Local residents gave him food and small gifts in return. In his position as Crossing-Sweeper he had become a little

self-important, some might even say smug. He expounded upon the rights and wrongs of life to all who would listen. He failed to notice that their numbers were dwindling! Few folk now offered him the chance to engage them in long conversations, but after a brief greeting hurried on their way. Only yesterday Grizzles had read a slow-moving snail a lecture on the sad modern habit of rushing everywhere. His captive audience, not unnaturally, agreed.

Grizzles looked up and saw the thin figure of a Shrew coming along the lane, obviously a stranger. He was wearing a mauve velour hat and carried a knobbly stick over his shoulder, from which hung a small bundle in a paisley handkerchief.

Grizzles was immediately struck by his bouncy, jaunty air and paused to watch as the Shrew approached, singing happily. His carefree gait was quite unlike the plodding tread of Snailsleap's more respectable denizens.

When he saw the Vole, the stranger stopped, rested his bundle on the ground and smiled. Grizzles was the first to speak. 'I can see that you are new to these parts. You'll be wanting directions?'

'No thank you,' replied the Shrew, 'that's one thing I never require.'

Grizzles' eyebrows rose with surprise.

The Shrew continued, 'I am not, you see, one of those tramps who shuttle back and forth on the same routes, year in and year out. No indeed, I am a professional Vagrant, a long-distance itinerant, a genuine Gentleman-of-the-road, Mr. Sweeper.'

'I prefer to be addressed as Crossing-Sweeper,' Grizzles retorted peevishly. 'It has the dignity which goes with my calling, whereas Sweeper is . . . is . . .'

'Reminiscent of a rather more menial mercantile,' interrupted the Shrew. And then, before Grizzles could recover, he continued, 'I am Valantine de Gasche, at your service,' and he swept off his feathered hat with a flourish and replaced it at an even more jaunty angle.

Grizzles began to tidy the brooms on his already immaculate barrow, to give himself time to think. The Vagrant irritated yet intrigued him. Out of the corner of his eye, Grizzles saw him take a silver snuff box from the small purse at his waist, place a pinch of snuff on the back of his hand, sniff delicately and then sneeze into a silk handkerchief.

Grizzles was then offered some snuff, but he refused, saying he preferred a pipe. He filled and lighted his best rosewood pipe, and in the companionable silence of these rituals he mellowed and invited Valantine de Gasche to share his midday meal.

'I suppose,' reflected Grizzles, 'you meet all kinds of interesting folk upon the road?'

'Yes indeed,' agreed Valantine, munching appreciatively into another sorrel sandwich. 'Why, I remember one day last summer, I was crossing a small stream and heard such a clamour, a cacophony of sound. I once heard a cicada in the New Forest. This was much the same, only more so.'

Grizzles had never heard of a 'cacophony'. It sounded dangerous but interesting. 'Yes, yes,' he said impatiently, 'what was it?'

The Lizard in the white velvet hat

AN UNEXPECTED SIGHT

Valantine took hours over the next mouthful.

'Cages!' he announced at last, with the air of one who has revealed all in a single word.

Grizzles leant limply back against the wheel of his barrow.

'Ah!' exclaimed Valantine, 'I see you are perplexed. Well, in a small bed of strawberry plants ... how I adore straw-berries ...'

'Oh *do* continue,' pleaded Grizzles.

'Well, there were *cages*, as I said, all different shapes and sizes. Made of wire, so beautiful and decorative you can't imagine. Now, I never took much notice of cages, but these were very unusual, something to look at, really splendid.'

He paused for breath and seeing Grizzles was following his discourse intently, he continued. 'They had turrets and balconies decorated everywhere with wire flowers and scrolls. Had I a home, I would have bought one, but in my way of life one can have few possessions.'

Grizzles mulled over this graphic description. In all his years as a crossing-sweeper, he had certainly never seen anything like that unexpected sight.

Grizzles was jolted from his reverie by Valantine continuing, '. . . and in them were Crickets and Grasshoppers!'

'That was the strange noise you heard!' cried Grizzles.

'Yes indeed, but that's not the end of the story. Sitting in the midst of them all was a Lizard. He had a rather foreign look and wore the most enchanting sombrero-like hat of white velvet.' Valantine sighed. 'Oh, to own such a perfectly *lovely* hat!'

Grizzles too sighed, and Valantine sighed again, a long sigh of covetousness. The opulence of such a splendidly, outrageously impractical hat struck them both quite dumb for some moments.

'Well, this Lizard fellow described himself as a Hawker, said he travelled up and down the country hawking these cages which he claimed to have made himself—not living like me, by

his wits, but by his skill and therefore quite an admirable Lizard in his way.'

Grizzles digested the oddly disturbing news of such strange characters wandering about, outside what he was beginning to realize was his own small world. He was jolted rudely from his musing by the fidgety Vagrant leaping up and saying that he had delayed too long already. He shook Grizzles cordially by the hand, reshouldered his small bundle, and was striding past the third clover plant before the still dazed Grizzles quite realized he was going.

The Vole's eyes followed the tiny darting figure as it reached the cross-roads. He replaced his sandwich basket on the barrow and when he looked up again the Shrew had gone—but not so the memory of their conversation.

For the rest of the day, Grizzles found himself unnecessarily tidying this and that, but always lingering towards the end of the lane where he had last seen the Vagrant. He himself had never ventured far along the wilder reaches over the hill. In fact, he realized with a shock that he had never been anywhere! Weeks, months and years had passed without Grizzles realizing it. He had become more rotund, his fur more greyish, his movements rather slower. It had all been so gradual that he had never noticed.

As the day drew to a close the Vole set off for home, pushing his barrow towards the little shack where he kept the various brooms and tools. For lack of somewhere better this had become his home.

He thought one thing was certain after such an unusual afternoon—nothing else exciting could possibly happen for a long while.

The Wood Mouse takes over the brooms

DREAMER IS RESCUED

The Vole's foretelling of peace and quiet was not to be. He had reached the path which ran alongside Sweetwater Pool when he heard a sobbing sound. Setting down his barrow and parting the trailing willow-tree branches, he saw a small Wood Mouse, wearing a crumpled hat and yellow handkerchief, standing in the water up to his waist and crying bitterly.

Grizzles was overcome with concern. 'Dear, dear me,' he said, 'Now, now, it's all right, I'll help you out.'

The only response was a further torrent of tears.

Near to the pool was a log of wood. Grizzles managed to roll this down into the water where it sank with a gurgling sound into the mud. The crinkled bark on the top rose above the water like a sleeping alligator, and along this causeway Grizzles scrambled until he reached the end and the Wood Mouse.

Feeling Grizzles' hands upon his arms, the Wood Mouse tried to speak, but his teeth were chattering too much with cold.

'Never mind,' said the Vole, as matter-of-factly as he could, 'Just step up on here and we'll soon have you on dry land.'

The Mouse's muddy feet slipped dangerously on the wet log, but after a few moments of anxious balancing, they both stood shakily on the bank. Grizzles helped the little Wood Mouse into the barrow and pushed him as fast as he could to his shack. Like all sensible animals, he always kept a store of dry wood by the chimney, so within minutes he had a cheerful crackling fire and a kettle of water hanging above.

Quickly and quietly Grizzles removed the Wood Mouse's sodden coat, washed his muddy legs and tucked him up in his own little bed.

Only when he had brought a cup of hot verbena and elder-flower tea did he ask any questions. He learned that the Wood Mouse had been very unhappy at home. He never seemed to do anything right, or to please his parents as his brothers and sisters did. He always managed to outrage his father and disappoint his mother, until one day he ran away.

Hungry and cold, he went aboard a narrow boat on a canal and while he was eating some crumbs under the table, the boat moved off! Fortunately, when the owners found the stowaway they gave him food in return for his help.

He travelled along the waterways, learning how to open and close the locks. Then one day he recognized the fields through which they passed and realized that he was not far from home. So he said goodbye to the river folk and scurried down the well-remembered paths until he reached his own front door. It was opened by a strange, unfriendly mouse who told him crossly that his family had gone away, no one knew where.

Grizzles was moved by the sad tale. He tucked the patch-work quilt around the little Wood Mouse and advised him to get a good night's sleep.

Next morning, after breakfast, the little Wood Mouse explained that he fell into the pool because he was crying and did not look where he was going. 'It's lucky you came along,' he said, wiggling his toes in the Vole's large warm slippers.

'Goodness me!' exclaimed Grizzles, 'I don't even know your name.'

'They call me D-D-Dreamer,' said the Wood Mouse.

'Dreamer,' repeated Grizzles, 'a very evocative name.'

'No, D-D-Dreamer,' insisted the Mouse.

'You've got such a lovely little house,' remarked Dreamer wandering about, picking up the ornaments on the shelves and looking at the pictures on the walls. He plumped up the cushion on Grizzles' armchair and straightened the rag rug by the fire.

'If only I had such a d-d-dear little home, I would always keep it clean and tidy. Just like you d-d-do,' Dreamer added hastily.

'I like a few bits and pieces about,' said Grizzles. 'It makes it homely, but not too many. To have too much of anything is asking for trouble.'

'Well now,' he said as he put on his green apron and hat, 'I'm just going to do a little sweeping. Would you like to come with me?'

'I should like to help you at whatever you d-d-do,' said Dreamer.

'Off I shall go in search of adventure'

THE VOLE MAKES A DECISION

So Grizzles fetched his barrow from the lean-to, and they set off. Dreamer was intrigued by the little barrow which was painted primrose yellow and rose pink with forget-me-not wheels lined-out in pink. Grizzles had painted sprays of flowers on the panelled sides and there was a spindle rack to rest the broom upon.

The Wood Mouse skipped along scurrying first to this side and then to that, asking endless questions, until the Vole became quite dizzy watching him. But he was so pleased that the little Mouse had recovered that he answered patiently. He told Dreamer of his interest in flowers and pointed out the variety that grew in Snailsleap.

When at last they stopped by a rotten branch which had fallen in the path, Dreamer begged to be allowed to 'do a little sweeping'. Grizzles readily agreed, for he was not averse to reclining against the barrow and mulling over the disturbing events of yesterday.

They were disturbing, he knew that . . . ever since the sudden appearance of Valentine de Gasche he had been aware of a growing restlessness deep within him.

He watched Dreamer as he attacked the arch of a bramble which had rooted on the road, threatening to trip some unwary traveller. Such enthusiasm would have been his a few days ago.

'S-s-such a lovely occupation you have. Who could fail to *want* t-t-to do it well? I can't remember ever having such a lovely morning as today.'

The Vole was indeed touched by his frank confession. What a pity, he thought, that the Wood Mouse seemed so suited to being a crossing-sweeper and yet wasn't one, while he, Grizzles, was beginning to feel that he was *not* suited to being one, and he was!

'D-d-do you th-think,' asked Dreamer, 'that you could help me be a crossing-sweeper where folk need one?'

Grizzles looked thoughtful, then said, 'Such positions are hard to find. It's no good setting up one's barrow where no-one has pride in keeping the paths clean. Round here, everyone who passes has a friendly word. I often have little presents given to me, and then there's the little shack, not to be sneezed at on a cold winter's night . . .'

The Wood Mouse interrupted him. 'Why mustn't you sneeze at the shack?'

Grizzles laughed. 'A figure of speech, my dear Dreamer, I mean one should appreciate it or value it, rather than the reverse.'

'Oh,' said the Wood Mouse, 'you are so very wise Mr. Grizzles.'

'Even if I had thought of retiring,' continued Grizzles, 'there was no one to carry on. But now that you've come along, I could perhaps hand over my brooms to you.'

'Mr. Grizzles!' cried the Mouse, dancing backwards into a spider's web. 'Would I have the little b–b–barrow as well?'

'Yes, why not?' smiled Grizzles, finding Dreamer's enthusiasm infectious. 'I've quite made up my mind to go travelling.'

Suddenly the Wood Mouse was sober. 'Where will you go?' he asked. 'You'll be like I was yesterday. You'll have no home,' he sniffed, a tear rolling from his eye at the thought of perhaps, after all, not being able to accept the Vole's offer.

'Don't distress yourself,' said Grizzles, 'I've quite made up my mind . . . it's Fate, that's what it is, you suddenly arriving just after another visitor I had. Anyway, once I've made up my mind to a thing, I hate delay, so tomorrow as ever is I shall put a few things together and off I shall go, in search of adventure.'

And even as he spoke he felt his spirits rise.

The Field Mouse's eyes brightened and she stepped forward

GRIZZLES MEETS GYPSY PEMBERLINE

When Grizzles awoke next morning, he lay and pondered if
he would be nervous when he no longer had a wall between himself and the world. Would Dreamer remember to tend the

garden? To hoe the weeds from his vegetable patch? 'Enough of these wiffly-waffly-dithery thoughts,' he told himself, resolutely jumping out of the armchair.

He showed the little Wood Mouse where the stream of clear water was, where to get the best holly wood for dry kindling, and where the birch trees grew to make new brooms, and he told him all he knew of Snailsleap Lane.

As Grizzles couldn't get all the things he felt he needed into a handkerchief like the Vagrant, he put them into a draw-string bag. He decided to take a warm rug, which he could also use as a coat.

Having said farewell to Dreamer, he hurried up the road to the signpost and turned left to Up. As he came to the edge of a meadow, he saw a Gypsy Flowerseller. When she saw the Vole, the Field Mouse's eyes brightened, and she stepped forward blocking the path.

'Mornin' to you, my fine gentleman,' she said, her eyes darting over his clothes to ascertain what manner of person he was, so that she would know what price to ask for her flowers. 'Buy a bunch of lovely flowers, Sir, to bring you luck.'

'Good morning to you, Mother,' said Grizzles, 'I'm afraid I am, what you might call, travelling light, and so have no use for your flowers. Today, I am joining the fraternity of the Gentlemen-of-the-Road.'

Even as she spoke, the flowerseller knew it was a losing battle. So she lowered her basket and replaced her clay pipe in her mouth.

Like many folk, Grizzles had never thought much about Gypsies, Romanies or the Travelling People, though he liked to *see* such colourful personages.

28

Pleased to pause awhile at the top of the long hill, he sat down and lighted his pipe. As there seemed to be no immediate rush of customers, the Flowerseller put down her willow arm-basket and also sat down.

'That's a fine pipe,' remarked Grizzles who had heard that some old Travelling women liked them, but had never before seen one being smoked. 'Won't you have some of my baccy?' he asked. His offer was accepted. The Gypsy Field Mouse, whose name was Pemberline, told him that if he put a leaf from the dock plant or wild cabbage in his pouch it would stop the tobacco going too dry. 'We make fine baccy from dried coltsfoot leaves,' she added.

They smoked in silence for a while and then Grizzles remarked, 'You are not from these parts, I take it?'

Pemberline chuckled. 'Every Romany is from *some-where*, my Son; people forgets we all have a birthplace, just like you. Most of us regard wherever that is as "our" country. We even speak with the local accent, not that anyone would notice that!'

Grizzles found it all very interesting and asked Pemberline if she would tell him more about the Travellers.

'Well, there are as many different kinds of Traveller as there are folk. Some never go very far from their home village, except to a Summer Fair, where we meet all our relations. As we may be anywhere at any time, it's hard to keep in touch, so we make arrangements to meet at a fair.'

Grizzles was surprised; he had thought that the Romanies never went to the same place twice.

'Of course,' continued Pemberline, 'there are those who travel all over the country; some go right across the sea and back, and never stay anywhere for long.'

'Life's very strange,' thought Grizzles, and he said aloud, 'One never knows what one will be when one grows up.'

'Hah!' exclaimed Pemberline, 'now there's a difference. There is never any question in the minds of the Travelling children. They just want to do what their parents do. We don't badger them to be this or that, as long as they learn how to make a living and keep a wife and children and look after their aged parents, which not all other folk do. What more need one ask?'

'I expect,' said Grizzles, 'you have a very free and easy life?'

'It ought to be free,' answered Pemberline, 'the idea is we are free, but in fact we are only free to *go*, seldom to stay.'

30

Grizzles looked puzzled, and Pemberline continued: 'Seeing us move about with no ties and having what the other folk think is freedom makes some of them jealous . . . Those Rabbits now, too afraid to leave their burrows and go to the next village, but let we kind of people stop a night or two near them and light a fire to cook supper! They soon send for Constable Mole to move us on. They buy our clothes pegs and baskets but forget that we need somewhere to stop and make them.'

Grizzles pondered much upon the unkindness of people and hoped he would find a more pleasant welcome.

'Well,' he said, 'I ought to be getting along.'

'You won't have to hurry now that you are a Gentleman-of-the-Road,' said Pemberline smiling. 'No rising early next day morning.'

'It was not my pocket but my stomach clock that I was taking more notice of,' said Grizzles, 'I am rather hungry.'

Few Romanies will pass a Vagrant or a Tramp, as Grizzles had now become, without offering him a bite to eat, so the Flowerseller took from the bottom of her basket a crusty loaf wrapped in a cloth, broke off a portion and gave it to Grizzles who thanked her gratefully.

At that moment, a stout figure made an appearance round the bend, puffing up the hill. The Flowerseller rose, straightened her pinna and resumed a business-like position across the path.

Grizzles spent that night snug and warm in a dry woodpile of twigs. The next day morning he was awakened by the singing of the hedgerow birds. He forgot for a moment where he was! Remembering the cheerful Vagrant, Valantine de Gasche, gave him encouragement, so shivering in the chilly morning air, he lighted a little fire. Later, when he was more experienced, he was to learn that the thing to do is to build a large fire like the Travelling people do. It warms one more quickly and is half the effort, as larger pieces of wood can be burned, which in turn last longer. On his little fire he placed a tin of water across two stones. It soon boiled and he dropped in some crushed oats which he greatly enjoyed.

The Green Frog in a fez hat showed his merchandise

ENTER THE VENDOR, DR. SILVERTONGUE

Later the next morning as he walked along a meandering
path, Grizzles began to grow very thirsty. He had used all his
water and could not find a stream. Seeing the sun glint on a little

window ahead, he turned down a tiny path rehearsing a speech which began very politely 'Good morning Madam' when, to his utter astonishment, he heard those *very* words spoken in a cajoling tone.

He halted. In front of the little house was a green frog wearing a fez hat, surrounded by bundles of rugs and carpets. These he was unrolling with a speed and flourish which fairly dazzled the eye, all the while talking non-stop of luxurious hand-knotted exotic masterpieces from the East which, due only to a series of personal misfortunes, he was able to offer to the lucky housewife for a mere fraction of their worth and original cost.

Here he paused for breath, and a shy shrew came forth from her house, attracted by the bright colours, like a moth to a flame.

Grizzles stood, unable to move, fascinated by the dexterity with which the Frog showed and replaced his merchandise, as indeed was the Lady of the House. Losing her fear of the caller, she became almost as enthusiastic as the Carpetseller, eventually buying two matching bedroom rugs and a runner for the hall!

The Green Frog had re-rolled his goods and was advancing upon the eavesdropping Vole before Grizzles realized it.

'Thank you, thank you, Friend,' said the Carpetseller-Vendor.

'Thank you?' queried Grizzles, somewhat perplexed.

'Why yes, why yes, I saw you there. Glad you had the good manners not to interrupt. It does not take much to frighten the dear ladies into retreating behind their net curtains.' The Frog shook his head sadly at the thought of such dire consequences.

'I remember,' continued the Frog, 'a friend had been calling all day and not a single brush or broom sold! Quite desperate he was. Then he saw a Shrew gardening. He hastened across her lawn on a line of stepping stones. To keep his balance, he raised his arms on high, clutching his long-handled brooms. On perceiving this unexpected apparition, the Shrew squealed loudly and vanished into the house.

Luckily the window was open, so when he got no response to his knocking he put his head in to reassure the lady, but she became even more terrified and closed the window on his head. He was rescued by the Postman, who could hardly stop laughing as he heard the poor fellow repeating plaintively 'Oh Madam, you are hurting my head.'

They had reached the road, but the Frog seemed in no hurry to lose his listener. 'You've no idea how rude some people can be. Quite often they close the door upon me before I even have a chance to tell them what I've come about! My own philosophy, learned from life and not books, I hasten to add, is "When one door closes, another opens".'

Grizzles congratulated the Frog on such a clever maxim.

'Goodness me,' exclaimed the Frog, introducing himself as Dr. Silvertongue, 'I fear I have interrupted your business.'

Grizzles told him that he had only been about to ask for a drink of water.

'Then follow me, Friend,' said Dr. Silvertongue, 'follow me, I am encamped just down the road, all conveniences including running water.' The Frog seemed hugely amused at his own remark. 'I should be delighted if you would care to dine with me? One meets so few itinerant folk.'

The Carpet Vendor's encampment was alongside a twinkling stream and he had a bender tent, made of hazelrods bent into the shape of half an apple, over which rugs and carpets were placed. In front were the ashes from his morning fire, which he rekindled. He placed a pot of victuals on top and soon they were eating an appetizing meal.

Grizzles found the Vendor vastly entertaining. Since leaving Snailsleap he had discovered how nice it could be to relax and let someone else do all the talking. What an erudite Frog he was!

He told Grizzles that he had not always been on his own but had once had a nice little wife.

'Ah well,' sighed the Frog resignedly, as Grizzles made himself comfortable by the fire for the night, 'I never could be at all domesticated. I fear I am a most unreliable Frog.'

As Grizzles drifted off to sleep he thought that folk were not always what they seemed and that sometimes the face they presented to the world concealed their true feelings.

Grizzles was glad he'd realized this, perhaps it would help him to be more understanding in the future.

The small Frog came into view over the brink of the hillock

MR. TINPAN'S TRAVELLING TROUBLES

The following day, Grizzles and Dr. Silvertongue went their separate ways.

Grizzles followed a path that ran for a time beside a small

stream, then led him upwards to higher ground. He climbed slowly humming a tune.

From the other side of the hillock there came a strange sound, music and yet not music—tantalising because it was impossible to recognize. Louder and louder it grew, a strange clanging, accompanied by a wheezing sound like some archaic organ bellows.

It reached a crescendo at the same moment that Grizzles reached the top. A curious sight came into his view over the brink of the hillock—a mound of coloured pots and pans, jangling and swinging from side to side, in the centre of which a small Frog was trying to keep his balance. Flying over his head was a lovely pink and gold Moth.

'Well,' he glared, 'don't just stand there, help me down with this.'

He wheezed and grunted as the Vole extricated him from the tins and pans and set them down among the yellow Pimpernel flowers. The furious little frog collapsed among the mauve Milkwort.

'Another Frog, so different from Dr. Silvertongue,' thought

38

Grizzles as the Frog, wheezing slightly less, introduced himself.

'Mr. Tinpan, they calls me, known h'all over the country h'as belongs to h'our Gracious Lady the Queen.' He paused for breath. 'There's not a kind of pan nor pot, round nor h'oval what I 'aven't 'andled. I deals in h'as diverse a company of pots h'as any cook may well dream of.'

Grizzles was still thinking of how best to answer, when Mr. Tinpan, regaining full power of his lungs by the minute, continued. 'I am not at all *partial* to this 'ere part of the country, not particular about it, you understand me?'

He regarded Grizzles somewhat balefully as though he suspected him of being a local resident, despite his now rather travel-worn appearance. Since his encounter with Dr. Silver-tongue, Grizzles felt more kindly disposed towards folk, so he really wished to show sympathy, but Mr. Tinpan scowled and continued, 'Never come this 'ere way without I 'ave some trouble,' and he looked even more cross. 'Last time some Tinkers threw h'all my stock in the river, said I was upsettin' their trade in pot-mendin'. Short-sighted lot, without my pots in the first place, they'd 'ave none to mend.'

'Indeed no,' rejoined the Vole, laughing to get the Frog into a more convivial frame of mind, but Mr. Tinpan only regarded the Vole and his immediate surroundings with mounting disdain.

'No, you certainly cannot be sure of meeting a decent class of folk in 'igh country. If it were not for a number of long-h'established customers, you wouldn't see me for dust.'

'It must be a very trying occupation and one quite without precedent,' said Grizzles, who wished to arrest the Frog's attention if not gain his respect by saying something grand.

Mr. Tinpan rose, fixed the Vole with his large protruding

eyes, and said, 'We can do without your "Precedents". H'all this country needs is more loyalty to 'Er Majesty the Queen. You'll be suggesting they serve cakes and ice-cream from Buckingham Palace next.'

After he had rested, the Vole helped the Frog to shoulder the pole from which hung his chattels. He accepted the assistance with a mere grunt and set off down the hill. Only when the Vole saw the Moth detach itself from the pink stonecrop flowers and follow the Frog, did he remember he had forgotten to ask about it. He stood looking after the retreating Frog, but couldn't bring himself to call out. 'Anyway, he probably wouldn't have heard above the sound of his own music,' thought the Vole, smiling.

A House Mouse clad all in black with a once rather fine top hat

A DARK STRANGER ON THE PATH

Grizzles spent many quiet days wandering down a flat valley, through which flowed a delightful stream burbling and gurgling over a bed of round stones which glowed in bright jewel colours under the water. Huge yellow Kingcups turned glistening golden basins to the sun, and delicate Dragonflies darted among the blue Forget-me-nots.

Gradually the stream widened into what his friend the Otter called 'a proper fishing river'. Graceful willows trailed their green hair over the swirling current. He lost count of the days and meandered like the river through Somerset and Devonshire.

One day, as he was just setting out along a sandy trail through clumps of Greater Celandine, he met a House Mouse clad all in black, with a once rather fine top hat. On one shoulder he carried a bundle of rod-like sticks and quite the funniest brooms that Grizzles had ever seen! Under the other arm he had a brush and a flask in a wicker holder. In his hand he carried a mysterious sack, black as his hat.

This Mouse told Grizzles that he was now in Cornwall, and begged him not to leave without making his way to the coast. 'You must see the sea, the finest sea anywhere,' said the Mouse, who introduced himself as Bartholemew Shaw, a master sweep. 'I once had six mice working under me, but now, trade isn't what it was.

'I know it's early for a Sweep to be about,' declared Bartholemew, 'but folks like to spring-clean now, so I tell them better make a thorough job of it and be ready for the late summer fires. With a clean chimney you'll have a roaring fire in no time.'

Grizzles nodded in agreement. 'Nothing is more aggravating than a chilly evening when the fire wont's draw. I never thought it could be because of soot.'

Bartholemew regarded Grizzles with amused pity. 'Chimneys get damp, same as folk. Now a chimney that's full of soot holds the damp, and a damp chimney won't 'courage the smoke.

'Well, talking won't buy me a loaf of bread today,' said the Master Sweep, 'unless I hurry on my way. Now don't forget to see the sea, it's a lovely wild coast. I can't bear to be away from it myself for long. Perhaps you will see one of the Fisher Rats.'

Grizzles said farewell to the Master Sweep. Some time later he looked in his little bag for his supper and found that he had none! He had so enjoyed his day finding the lily-like flowers of the square-stalked Garlic and the blue Spring Squill and observing new landscapes, that he had quite forgotten that he was dependent on the kindness and charity of other folk, and had passed the last few pathside dwellings with scarcely a glance!

He was chiding himself for his stupidity when he saw an old Mouse, shawl over head, go up a path and into a little house hidden in a thorn tree. Grizzles' hopes brightened, he hurried after her and tapped on the door.

Feet scuffled inside, the door opened a tiny crack, but before Grizzles could open his mouth a voice said 'Go away, I never buy anything at the door.'

'Indeed, Madam,' replied Grizzles, 'but I'm not selling anything.' He waited expectantly, but the voice repeated, 'Go away.'

So Grizzles went supperless to bed, wrapped in his rug-coat.

Round the bend came a Field Vole with a brass bell

THE KINDLY TOSS-UP PIEMAN

Hunger pains awoke him the next morning, so he rose early and washed in the dewy grass, took up his bundles and with the exciting prospect of seeing the sea, he took a by-way across some stony ground. He had heard tales of travellers in the desert who see mirages: they think they see what they most desire to see, an oasis with water. Grizzles was very hungry and the thing he most fancied was a pie. It had been a considerable time since he had had the luck to be given a pie. And so he thought it was a kind of mirage when he fancied he could smell one. At such an hour in the morning he knew it to be impossible, certainly not a hot pie.

So imagine his astonishment when round the bend came a Field Vole dressed in a starched white apron with a shallow tray on his head, and carrying a brass bell. From the tray came the unmistakable aroma of freshly-baked *hot pies*!

The Field Vole's name was Trevellyan. He said he was 'Cornish born and bred' and he took no end of trouble to tell Grizzles all the names of the plants which were new to him. Grizzles said he had never seen anything so pretty as the pink Thrift, like a miniature carnation growing in mounds of all sizes on the tops of the stone walls and even spreading to the ground in odd corners among the stones, and that he loved the creamy white Marine Campion and the bright blue Alcanet.

Trevellyan told Grizzles that he was a Toss-up Pieman and that he and his wife were up most nights baking pies, and that he was called such a funny name, not because he tossed the pies in the air like one does a pancake, but because it was an old custom to toss a coin for a pie. If you called out the side which landed upper-most when it fell to the ground then you had won yourself a free pie! If you lost your gamble you paid for the pie, of course. The lure of this very acceptable possibility gave the Toss-up Pieman a fine trade.

'Out of the goodness of my heart and the kindness of my

spirit, I offer you a free pie if you can but call the coin,' said the Pieman, as if suddenly sensing Grizzles' great hunger.

Grizzles thought it a very splendid idea, one of the most sensible he'd ever heard of, so he was very mortified to discover that he did not have a single coin. The kindly Toss-up Pieman said, 'Never mind, I wouldn't want you to remember us as inhospitable folk, so please accept this pie, with my compliments.'

Grizzles thought there could hardly be a better start to a day than munching a pie, walking down a cliff-path to the sound of the soaring Skylarks, with the sight of the white Gulls cutting the blue sky with their sickle wings. Grizzles waved goodbye to Trevellyan, who smiled and waved his little bell.

Suddenly there between two cliffs was a horizon of immense flatness. The sun sparkled on a constantly moving surface, a stretch of water so vast that it seemed to Grizzles to have taken over the whole world, and he glanced behind him to make sure he wasn't surrounded! Rolling waves of greeny-blue water threw up little white feathers of spume as they rose from the surface, arched, curved gracefully downwards, ran towards the land and merged again with the ocean. Greatly wondering, he made his way down the uneven cliff path and found himself in a most delightful sheltered cove, of secret rock pools full of all kinds of strange and wonderful sea-life, all living their secret salty lives. He was entranced, to say the least.

The Grinder was a handsome Field Mouse with black whiskers

GRANDFATHER AVONDOVE'S BARROW

Grizzles idly watched a little boat which appeared round a promontory and began to head towards the shore. Out climbed a friendly Fisher Rat who showed Grizzles where to find edible seaweed. He said he always came ashore for his 'tea', which was a mixture of mallow, toadflax and periwinkle leaves with flowers of the sea pink and red clover. The flames under the bleached drift-wood burnt white and invisible in the sun, the water hissed and bubbled in the Fisher Rat's black tin kettle. The Vole declared he hadn't tasted any better tea anywhere, which pleased the Cornish Rat immensely.

Grizzles thought of staying a while and pointed to an inviting-looking cave, but the Rat shook his head and indicated high-water marks up the cliff which showed the cave would flood at high tide. So he made his way up the cliff path until he found a safe cave. Here he made his home for a week, drinking the fresh water that trickled down the hill in a streamlet, full of watercress.

After many happy weeks in the West Country, he made his way, by a lucky ride on a haywain, up the Somerset coast into Worcestershire. He was quite surprised to see so much flat country after the Devonshire hills, and the cultivated fields of vegetable and fruit. It reminded him of home. He thought about Snailsleap and wondered how Dreamer was getting along and whether he was looking after the paths properly.

Then, as he walked along, he was further reminded of home. He noticed a row of little doors of all different colours and sizes. Opposite these were plants of Wild Cabbage, Wild Turnip, Yellow Archangel, Goatsbeard and a late flowering Keys of Heaven. These varying shades of yellow made a bright ring, in the centre of which a pink and gold barrow glittered with such brilliance that Grizzles' breath was quite taken away. Every inch of wood was carved in petal and leaf designs. A dainty spindle-rail bordered the top. The sides and front were decorated with elaborate painted scrolls. There was a frontispiece which was the finest example of the craftman's art that he had ever seen.

As he moved closer, he saw the owner, Mr. Avondove, climb up onto the little seat perched across the two handles and begin to work the treadle which, by way of a belt, drove the spindle which was the grindstone. This in turn sharpened the blades to the accompaniment of sparks and stone-grinding noises. Mr. Avondove, the Grinder, was a handsome Field Mouse, with fine black whiskers.

'I can see that you are admiring my barrow,' observed Mr. Avondove, trying the sharpness of a knife on a blade of grass.

'I am indeed,' replied Grizzles with feeling, 'I have a modest little barrow, or had when I was a Crossing-Sweeper —made it myself.'

The Field Mouse regarded him with more interest. 'Then you'll appreciate more than most that every inch of gold is real gold-leaf. It was my Grandfather's barrow. Many of the early knife-grinders' barrows had quaint lettering, much of it misspelt, like "Dissors Grinded" or "Dissors Sharped", so that people often called us "Dissors Grinders".'

'I expect it must help your trade, folk coming out to admire it and then finding work for you.'

At that moment two young voles came up with a pair of shears and some scissors, so Grizzles said goodbye to the Grinder.

The sky became cloudy and the fine weather gave way to rain. A kind Hedgehog gave Grizzles shelter for the night and while they ate a good supper, Grizzles gave such a colourful account of his wanderings that his host was tempted to take to the roads also!

The Fat Dormouse said there was no finer life than that of a Packman

THE VOLE MAKES A FRIEND

Next day morning he set off alone on a sunny road with a new pair of boots given him by the thoughtful Hedgehog. Fragile butterflies flew among Pyramid Bugle and Rough-Headed

Poppies as he walked along a high path. He glanced down into the valley below and saw a figure walking along a canal towpath, carrying something on his back and with both hands loaded with bags. 'Another Gentleman-of-the-Road,' thought Grizzles hopefully, and decided to make his way down hill at the first opportunity.

However, while he was content with a measured tread, the figure below sped along; it looked as though he would miss him altogether. But at a bridge across the canal where the paths converged, his quarry paused to rest upon the parapet. Grizzles caught him up.

The two itinerants introduced themselves. Grizzles learned that he was Trelawney Fat Dormouse, and a Packman. Not that he was especially fat, but there are Dormice and Fat Dormice, another name for which is Edible Dormice, but as you can imagine, he did not at all like the sound of that!

The Packman was working his way through the Midlands selling his wares, which were vanity items, laces, trimmings, calico, brushes and combs. The two wayfarers liked each other at once.

Trelawney said that his ancestors had come to this country in nineteen hundred and two from Switzerland, a country of high mountains and beautiful flowers. Every spring, he set off on his travels following the trade of his family. He said he thought there was no finer life than that of a Packman.

'Where do you sleep?' asked Grizzles.

Trelawney said that he put up at an Inn or Farmhouse and paid 'in kind'.

'What manner of payment is that?' asked Grizzles.

'My visit,' explained Trelawney, 'often means a new dress for the farmer's wife, so I give her a length of material to make a new petticoat for it, in return for which she gives me a night's lodging.'

Grizzles remarked that the Packman must take heart from the fact that his pack could only get lighter!

Trelawney made a good sale at the end of their first day travelling together. With the farmer's permission they climbed up into his cosy hayloft and, after dining on a meal of garlic bread and goat's cheese, fell fast asleep. The next day morning, his new friend told Grizzles of the great Hiring Fairs where, before folk were able to advertise, they could hire a shepherd, or a maid, or any person who wished to gain employment. Boys who wanted to learn a trade that their fathers could not teach them, could there find someone who would take them as an apprentice.

Folk wore the costume which was associated with their calling, like a butcher wears a striped apron. Shepherds would carry a crook, farm hands wear a smock, a carter carry a whip and so on, so that each could be recognised.

Grizzles enjoyed his conversation with Trelawney, but he liked the walking rather less. Trelawney had no eye for the flowers of the hedgerow nor appreciation of insects, unlike Grizzles. Grizzles would lose all account of time, investigating anything which aroused his curiosity, thus lagging behind the energetic Trelawney whose effervescent moods and boundless vitality he found a trifle trying. Trelawney, on the other hand, was irritated by Grizzles' 'dawdling', he wanted to 'get on'.

One day as they walked in companionable silence, Grizzles, keeping abreast not without effort, pondered how one could find oneself propelled into an immediate friendship but then discover a difference of outlook which prevented perfect companionship.

So it was inevitable that they eventually parted company, or as the Packman said, 'made two roads of it'. They separated amicably, albeit rather sadly, with much waving of hands.

The Bank Vole sold delicious strawberries

GRIZZLES RESCUES A TIP-CART

Despite Grizzles managing the practicalities of the way-farer's life and his great enjoyment of exploring, he was beginning to be aware of a feeling of unease. He felt a strange mood upon him, as he gathered up his belongings one day after breakfast. In the clear sky was a promise of another lovely summer's day. A tiny singing Skylark rose and fell as though on a piece of elastic. But Grizzles couldn't seem to feel the same excitement at setting out on the day's adventure. When he came to a fork in the road he had difficulty in making up his mind which direction to take.

Then he heard a sound from the left, and he took that path. As he progressed he could distinguish a few cross words. Soon he saw the cause. A tip-cart had one of its tiny wheels caught among the brambles. Struggling to extricate it, but with no success, was a Bank Vole in a yellow dress with a huge hat of white lace, so piled high with decorations that Grizzles wondered how she managed to keep it on!

Grizzles rushed forward, 'Allow me,' he said, as with a few tugs he released the cart, from which punnets filled with delicious-looking strawberries were offered for sale.

The Bank Vole sank down upon the grass, her bonnet askew.

'Thank you so much, young man,' she gasped, 'I am Star-Lena Penfold.'

Flattered to be called 'young', Grizzles too sat down. Before long, he found himself telling this motherly-looking Vole all about his life as a Crossing-Sweeper and his adventures. Star-Lena Penfold listened sympathetically. He confided that he could in no way account for being less able to enjoy his wanderings.

Without hesitation the Strawberry Seller declared, 'Home Sickness.'

Grizzles looked puzzled and told her he no longer had a home.

'That makes no difference,' said Star-Lena. 'You must be the kind of person who should have one.'

Grizzles looked thoughtful, then he asked the Strawberry Seller for her advice. She said he should return to his crossing-sweeping, but instead of never going anywhere he should take a long holiday now and then.

Grizzles thought this a most excellent idea and thanked Star-Lena. They ate a pleasant lunch of apple pie and strawberries and then Grizzles resumed his way, his gloom and sadness vanished. The journey back to Snailsleap, like most return journeys, took no time at all. He grew excited as he recognised the tall trees of Romany Wood, the cross roads of Up and Along, and then the narrow path of Snailsleap Lane.

Never had a stretch of country seemed so beautiful and the Vole's eyes filled with tears as he hastened along. When at last he reached the little shack, he found that Dreamer was astonished but delighted to see him. All was in order, exactly the same as he remembered, except that the little Wood Mouse had given the shabby front door a new coat of yellow paint.

They talked far into the night as Grizzles told of his adventures, of how he became homesick and didn't know it, and of how he felt that he could now appreciate his own little bit of the world. The Wood Mouse said that he had enjoyed being a Sweeper, but that he had become rather fidgety of late, letting his attention wander from his task as he dreamt of far away places.

As you can imagine, Grizzles felt very relieved that the

little Wood Mouse did not want to remain as Crossing-Sweeper.

'You see, Grizzles,' said Dreamer, 'I shall always b-b-be very grateful for all you've d-d-done for me, but I'd really like to see a little more of the world.'

So the little Wood Mouse went off in search of adventure, full of youthful curiosity and optimism, promising faithfully to come again and see Grizzles, whom he looked upon as an adopted Uncle.

The Vole settled down to his sweeping once again, and to laying in a store of winter firewood. To all the folk who enquired next day, he said 'I am very pleased that I went away, but I am even more pleased to be back home again,' and he repeated it softly to himself, 'Home.'